BOOK ANALYSIS

Written by Steve MacGregor

The Curious Incident of the Dog in the Night-Time

BY MARK HADDON

BrightSummaries.com

MARK HADDON

ENGLISH NOVELIST AND POET

- **Born in Northampton, England** in **1962.**
- **Notable works:**
  - *Agent Z and the Killer Bananas* (2001), children's book
  - *The Talking Horse and the Sad Girl and the Village Under the Sea* (2005), poetry collection
  - *A Spot of Bother* (2006), novel

Mark Haddon is a contemporary English writer, playwright, screenwriter, poet and cartoonist who has produced award-winning works for both adults and children. He was educated at Oxford University and Edinburgh University, gaining a Master's degree in writing, and he initially wrote books for children, often self-illustrated. As well as seeing his own work for children adapted by the BBC, he has also adapted other writers' work for television. Haddon is a vegetarian, an atheist and a long-time supporter of animal rights.

THE CURIOUS INCIDENT OF THE DOG IN THE NIGHT-TIME

A MYSTERY STORY TOLD BY A YOUNG MAN WITH A VERY DIFFERENT VIEW OF THE WORLD

- **Genre:** novel (mystery/family drama)
- **Reference edition:** Haddon, M. (2008) *The Curious Incident of the Dog in the Night-Time.* New York: First Vintage Books Edition.
- **1st edition:** 2003
- **Themes:** independence, perception, coping with loss, family relationships

The Curious Incident of the Dog in the Night-Time is the story of 15-year-old Christopher Boone, who attempts to solve the mystery of who killed Wellington the poodle with a pitchfork. The story is narrated by Christopher, who has an unnamed condition which affects his perception of the world around him. This condition is not defined or named in the novel, but it exhibits many of the characteristics of a form of autism or of Asperger's syndrome. The novel takes us on Christopher's journey of self-discovery set against a backdrop of broken families in suburban England, with events described as they are seen through the eyes of this unusual teenager.

The book examines contemporary issues such as divorce, parenting and separation and was hugely well received on publication, winning, amongst other accolades, the 2003 Whitbread Book of the Year award and selling more than two million copies. Initially written as Mark Haddon's first book for adults, it was simultaneously published as a young adult book – the adult and young adult versions were identical other than the cover.

SUMMARY

THE DOG THAT DID NOT BARK

The novel begins with our protagonist and narrator, 15-year-old Christopher Boone, discovering the body of Wellington, a large, black poodle who belongs to his neighbour Mrs. Shears. The dog has been stabbed to death with a pitchfork on Mrs. Shears' lawn. Christopher decides to solve this killing and write a book about it, following in the footsteps of one of his heroes, Sherlock Holmes. The title itself is a quote from *The Adventure of Silver Blaze*, a Sherlock Holmes short story, and like one of these classic mysteries, this seemingly simple death later reveals a web of lies and intrigue as the investigation progresses.

Christopher recounts the story through his own eyes, though he is sometimes aided and sometimes hampered in his investigation because he has a mild disability. This means that he cannot understand the world in abstract terms and cannot always understand the more subtle motivations of others or comprehend normal social cues.

ARRESTED DEVELOPMENT

The police are called, and initially seem to wonder if Christopher may have been responsible. Christopher reacts to their arrival at the scene of the crime by hitting one of them because he does not understand what the policeman is asking him to do. He is taken into custody because he and the policeman do not understand each other's motivations: "I do not like people shouting at me...I do not know what is going to happen" (Chapter 5). This short scene means that the reader is quickly made aware of the problems that Christopher faces in human interactions, and also of the difficulties for those who have to live with him in coping with his behaviour. He is released after his father, Ed Boone, appears to explain the situation. We are given our first glimpse of their relationship, when his father calms him and uses special techniques to explain the situation to his son.

THE BOY DETECTIVE

On the suggestion of a teacher at his special school, Siobhan, this investigation becomes an assignment - the book that we are reading is the manuscript prepared by Christopher for school. He is aided in his writing with advice from his teacher, who is also supporting him in his attempt to take a maths A level and to fulfil his dream of going to university. We learn that Christopher and his father are alone after his mother has fallen ill and died in hospital. This surprised Christopher, as she had seemed to him to be active and healthy.

His investigations propel him into the world of adults, which to him seems chaotic and emotionally messy and confusing. Whenever he attempts to find the truth of what has happened, he meets resistance from his father, Mrs. Shears and other neighbours, but he continues to write up what he finds. He leaves the book in view of his father, who is very angry when he reads it and forbids him to continue to play detective, but Christopher continues in secret, having justified his deceit in concrete terms that satisfy him.

THE TRUTH IS WRITTEN LARGE

The book disappears, presumably hidden by his father, but Christopher searches and finds it, concealed under a box of letters written by his mother to him over a long period of time. Christopher is very confused: he had been told by his father that his mother was dead, but some of the letters he finds have been written recently. Initially, he is reluctant to read the letters: "I wondered whether I should open the envelope... But then I reasoned that it was addressed to me so it belonged to me so it was OK to open it" (Chapter 149). Christopher realises that, in fact, his mother is not dead but has actually left him and his father to live with Mr. Shears, the husband of Wellington's owner, with whom she has been having an affair.

The letters shift the narrative perspective from first to third person and we learn of his mother´s reasons for leaving, her struggles to cope with the life she had previously led and how much she misses her son and wants him to visit her. Despite never getting an answer, she has continued to write to him regularly. In shock, Christopher faints and is discovered by his dad surrounded by the letters.

His father tries to explain his motivations for hiding the letters, saying he felt it would be easier than forcing Christopher to cope with rejection. He apologises, saying that he was trying to protect Christopher from feelings of abandonment. He also confesses to killing the dog as well. This pivotal scene changes him in his son's (and consequently, the reader's eyes) from a well-meaning widower to villain of the book, the antagonist to Christopher and the destroyer of all of his hopes and dreams. Like Christopher, we now have to reassess what we thought was the reality of their lives.

THE RUNAWAY

Christopher is now deathly afraid of his father and decides that he cannot stay with him. He hides in his room, refusing to see or speak to his dad as he believes he is a killer and that he is himself in grave danger. We see him withdraw and follow his father's futile attempts to reconnect with him, all of which end in failure. Christopher decides that his only logical course of action is to go to London and to find and live with his mother.

He embarks on a mini road trip that enables him to come of age in classic style, just as so many other heroes do on similar road trips in other novels from *The Adventures of Huckleberry Finn* by Mark Twain to *On the Road* by Jack Kerouac. On the way, Christopher must overcome difficulties with finding his way, both practically and symbolically. He struggles to come to terms with communication with other people as well as finally learning to care for his own needs.

REUNION

Christopher finds his mother living in a small flat in London, and sits and waits for her to return from work. She is shocked and delighted to see him but her partner is not, and although his mother tries to balance the needs of her lover and her son, she loses her job and Christopher becomes hysterical about the fact that he may not be able to take his maths A level. Ed turns up to see them, but Christopher is so terrified of him and the situation between the men turns so unpleasant that he is forced to leave. After a particularly bad incident, Christopher's mother throws out Mr. Shears and heads back with Christopher to their old family house. Ed works on regaining the trust of his son, finally buying him a puppy, and they gradually begin to rebuild their relationship. Christopher's mother gets a new job and a new flat, and Christopher takes his A level maths and passes with an A.

By the end of the book, mysteries are solved and the family is moving forward. This does not happen in a neat, tidy way, but through the chaos each member is finding a new way to connect and to make sense of their lives.

CHARACTER STUDY

CHRISTOPHER JOHN FRANCIS BOONE

Christopher is a 15-year-old maths prodigy and the protagonist of this story. He is the narrator of most of this novel, and we see the action principally through his eyes. Christopher has an unspecified disability, probably Asperger's syndrome, which means that he has to attend a special school, and he struggles for social acceptance and to make sense of the world around him: "I find it hard to imagine things which did not happen to me" (Chapter 7). Christopher finds changes in his routine extremely challenging and approaches life with logic and in concrete terms, using these characteristics to try to solve the mystery of who killed the eponymous dog.

As the book progresses, we see him attempt to move towards greater independence and into adulthood, whilst trying to cope with the shifting relationships of the adults around him and his changing views of them. He narrates in a clear, honest and unflinchingly objective style that is sometimes brutal about other people's feelings and emotions, and which forces the reader to confront not only the frequent dishonesty of social conventions, but also their necessity in the smooth running of human relationships.

ED BOONE

Christopher's father is a heating engineer and his sole carer since his wife left the family. Sometimes impatient and quick to anger, Ed Boone struggles to understand his son and to juggle the needs of work and fatherhood. As a father, he shows insight and creativity in dealing with Christopher's complex needs. We later learn that he has lied to Christopher by telling him that his mother is dead rather than admitting that she has left the family. This lie causes a schism in his relationship with his son. His later confession to being the killer of the dog because he was angry about his burgeoning relationship with Mrs. Shears coming to an end makes Christopher fear him: "Father had murdered Wellington. That meant he could murder me" (Chapter 167). Ed Boone is cast as the antagonist and villain of the piece at this point, but actually we also feel that he may have had reasons apart from jealousy and anger for concealing of the truth from Christopher.

These confessions propel us to the second part of the book, where Ed attempts to deal with the fallout of this event and tries to rebuild his relationship with Christopher.

JUDY BOONE

Judy is Christopher's mother, whom the reader initially believes has tragically fallen ill and died in hospital. Christopher recalls her as loving, impulsive and protective, although his reaction to her death also strikes the reader as oddly flat in affect. Later we learn that she is not dead but has left with her neighbour Mr. Shears, with whom she is having an affair. She briefly takes over narration in the novel, the only other character who does so, through the letters that she has been writing to her son and which Christopher discovers hidden. She says that she left for idealistic reasons, but the reader gets the impression that she may have been depressed and finding her son hard to cope with, and that his special needs had put a terrible strain on her marriage. Later events in the novel show her to be resilient, independent, resourceful and fiercely devoted to Christopher as she copes with his unexpected reappearance in her life.

MRS. SHEARS

Eileen Shears is the Boones' neighbour, and it is her dog that is found stabbed with a pitchfork. We learn little about her, though we are told that she had a relationship with Mr. Boone after her husband left with his wife, but that she found Christopher too hard to manage and ended the relationship, and she now wants nothing to do with the family. The killing of her dog, Wellington, is the main dramatic incident in the story.

MR. SHEARS

Mr. Shears is living with Christopher's mother after they began an affair and left their respective partners. He does not either need or want Christopher in their family unit and has no understanding of his condition or the relationship that he has with his mother. His negative reaction to Christopher's reappearance in their lives drives the story of the Boone family forward to its conclusion.

SIOBHAN

Siobhan is Christopher's teacher and significant carer at his special school, who encourages him to write a book and gives him advice on how to make it engaging for the reader. For example, she advises him to leave maths puzzles out of the narrative. Through her reported words in the book, we learn how she gives Christopher coping strategies for life and filters the world in ways that enable him to understand it more clearly. Siobhan becomes the reader's eyes and ears as the observer of Christopher's actions and words.

ANALYSIS

DETECTIVE FICTION

This novel is a detective story, albeit an unusual one, a genre characterised by:

- a crime, often a murder;
- an investigation;
- the revelation of deeper secrets;
- a professional or amateur detective, often a maverick or a person who is unusual or distinctive in some way.

The crime in this case is the killing of Wellington the poodle in a particularly brutal and horrific manner, which provides the story's dramatic impetus. It is this crime that Christopher decides to investigate in the manner of his hero Sherlock Holmes, by interviewing witnesses and searching for clues: "This is a murder mystery novel" (Chapter 7). As a detective, our protagonist follows closely in the footsteps of other fictional investigators such as Agatha Christie's Hercule Poirot and Ian Rankin's John Rebus, in having a maverick and unconventional approach and view of the world. He has this unconventional approach to life because of his own personality and mental processes. As he continues to probe more deeply, the secrets of his own family and neighbours are revealed to him and, as in all classic detective fiction, it becomes apparent that motivations are more complex than they originally appear.

THEMES

A major theme in this novel is a struggle for independence. Christopher's journey towards adulthood and independence reflects that of many teenage protagonists, such as Harry Potter in the eponymous books by J. K. Rowling, and Holden Caufield in *A Catcher in the Rye* by J. D. Salinger, as they overcome problems and struggle to make sense of the world around them: "I want my name to mean me" (Chapter 29). For Christopher this is an especially difficult journey because of his lack of understanding of other people, social mores and abstract thought. His investigation means he has to speak to strangers and make decisions about his next steps. The A level maths exam also becomes a symbol of his path to independence, as it is his key to moving away from home. During his road trip to London, a challenging experience for him, he faces obstacles to reach his destination. His mother and father also make moves towards their own independence as they struggle to make sense of their decisions and their responsibilities.

Christopher perceives the world in a very different way than the reader or the other characters, and this theme of perception is explored in the novel: "I think prime numbers are like life. They are very logical but you could never work out the rules, even if you spent all your time thinking about them" (Chapter 19). Reflecting Christopher's fascination, the 51 short chapters in the book are numbered using prime numbers rather than the more traditional sequential numbers.

Haddon uses interesting digressions to explore his protagonist's unusual perception of the universe around him, and incidents such as his arrest by the police at the start of the book and the transport police later on show the gulf between his view of the world and that of others, and how this propels dramatic scenes in the book forward: "That was because when I was little I didn't understand about other people having minds" (Chapter 163). Haddon forces us to enter the narrator's world by using first person narrative perspective and makes us question what is real and how much of what we regard as normal behaviour is actually based on social norms and expectations.

LOSS AND THE UNTIDINESS OF LIFE

Many of the characters in the book are coping or are forced to cope with loss. Christopher believes that his mother is dead, and then must later come to terms with the fact that she has chosen to leave him. Later, he and his father lose their relationship with each other, and his father has already lost his relationship with his wife and then with his lover. Mrs. Shears has also lost her husband, her dog and a burgeoning affair. Even their other neighbour is a widow. Mrs. Boone has chosen to leave, but her feelings of loss about her son are clear in her letters to him, where the narrative perspective shifts to the second person. Trust, dreams and love are all challenged, lost and sometimes refound during the novel.

Closely tied to this is the idea that real life is not tidy or logical: "Then he said, I did it for your good, Christopher. Honestly I did. I never meant to lie" (Chapter 157). It is chaotic and messy and, despite the fact that Christopher uses strategies to try to impose order and control on his environment and relationships, he is not successful. He is frequently undermined in this at home, at school, during his investigations and in his dreams about a new life with his mother. The conclusion of the novel offers no really neat solutions. It is not even clear if Christopher will be able to fulfil his dreams of going to university. While it may be tempting to hope for a family reconciliation, the actual resolution of the family unit seems to offer contemporary resonance and a reality which readers can relate to.

LOOKING FOR ORDER IN THE UNIVERSE

Most of the book is written from the protagonist's perspective, and Haddon uses language effectively to give us insight into the mind of an unusual young man. Most sentences are short, begin with the personal pronoun and are declarative. "I like dogs. You always know what a dog is thinking. It has four moods. Happy, sad, cross and concentrating" (Chapter 5). We are forced to deal with the words in concrete terms and not to look for hidden meaning beneath them, in just the same way that Christopher responds to the words of others. The structure and content of the language very much illuminate Christopher´s personality. The reader not only gets to see the world through his unique eyes, but also has the chance to question their own perception of the world. For example, Christopher challenges religious belief when he says: "I think people believe in heaven because they don't like the idea of dying, because they want to carry on living" (Chapter 61). When he does add more complex sentences, this allows the reader to see that although he thinks in a concrete way, Christopher is not a person of limited intelligence or understanding.

Repetition is also used to show how Christopher is a precise thinker and to reveal how he uses concrete words to create order and security in his world. Christopher does not understand metaphors or similes, so he does not use these in his writing, adding to the simplicity and directness of the text.

Haddon also uses maths, science and logic puzzles throughout the book as a way of illuminating the fact that Christopher likes to see the universe in an ordered way, as this makes him feel secure. These are also used to order and explain more complex ideas for him, such as on the train when he uses Conway's Riddle to pass the time. They enable him to make order from chaos and also give him security at times when he cannot understand what is happening around him or assess the emotions of others.

Sherlock Holmes is Christopher's fictional detective hero, in part because Holmes also sees the world in concrete terms and seems untroubled by emotions. Moreover, Holmes uses logic to solve mysteries, something that accords with Christopher's desire not just to solve the killing of Wellington, but also to try to understand the world and the actions of others in logical terms. Even the title of the novel reflects these ideas. In the short story from which the title is taken, Holmes uses this phrase to allude to something that should have happened but had not, and this apparent lack proves to be very significant in the solution of the mystery. In this novel, one of the central events in Christopher's life is the death of his mother. Only later in the book do we learn that this actually has not happened, and this fact becomes very significant both in the solution to the mystery of the killing of Wellington the poodle, and in Christopher's life more generally.

FURTHER REFLECTION

SOME QUESTIONS TO THINK ABOUT…

- The title is a quote from a Sherlock Holmes short story. In what ways are Holmes and Christopher similar?
- What do you think the drawings add to your understanding and appreciation of the novel?
- How far has Christopher actually moved towards real independence by the end of the book?
- How much influence do you believe that his condition had on the breakdown of his parents' relationship? Explain your answer.
- Does the lack of another consistent perspective on events in this novel add to or detract from your reading?
- "All the other children at my school are stupid. Except I'm not meant to call them stupid, even though this is what they are" (Chapter 71). In what ways are social conventions upheld or undermined in the book?

- What do you think will happen next in the lives of the characters?
- The setting is recognisably England but the book was a global success. Why do you think this is?
- Do you consider this a book most appropriate for adults, young adults or children? Why?
- Which parts of the book resonate with your own life and experiences?
- This novel does not provide any physical description of Christopher – we are not told if he is tall or short, fat or thin, fair or dark. Why do you think the author chose to do this?
- In an interview about this book in *The Guardian* newspaper in 2004, author Mark Haddon said: "Reading is a conversation. All books talk. But a good book listens as well." What do you think he means by this?

We want to hear from you!
Leave a comment on your online library
and share your favourite books on social media!

FURTHER READING

REFERENCE EDITION

- Haddon, M. (2008) *The Curious Incident of the Dog in the Night-Time*. New York: First Vintage Books Edition.

REFERENCE STUDIES

- Haddon, M. (2004) B is for bestseller. *The Guardian*. [Online]. [Accessed 5 December 2018]. Available from: <https://www.theguardian.com/books/2004/apr/11/booksforchildrenandteenagers.features3>

ADDITIONAL SOURCES

- *The Memoirs of Sherlock Holmes*, the anthology of Sherlock Holmes short stories by Sir Arthur Conan Doyle (English novelist, short story writer, poet and essayist, 1858 – 1930) which includes *The Adventure of Silver Blaze,* in which Holmes refers to "the curious incident of the dog in the night-time", is in the public domain and available for download at the Project Gutenberg site at: <http://www.gutenberg.org/ebooks/834>

ADAPTATIONS

- A stage adaptation of this work written by Simon Stephens (English playwright, born in 1971) was first performed at the National Theatre in London. This stage play was filmed and an edited version was released for theatrical screening in September 2012. The stage play later transferred first to the Apollo Theatre and then to the Gielgud Theatre in London. This adaptation has also been performed in a number of theatres in the US. An adaptation and translation into Spanish was performed at the Teatro de los Insurgentes in Mexico City in 2014. In the same year, an adaptation and translation into Hebrew was performed in Tel Aviv.
- The film rights to this work were purchased in 2011 by actor Brad Pitt and film producer Brad Grey. It was also announced that Steven Kloves, the writer of the screenplays for most of the Harry Potter films, had been commissioned to write a screenplay. To date, no timescale has been announced for the production of a film adaptation.

www.brightsummaries.com

Ebook EAN: 9782808016070

Paperback EAN: 9782808016087

Legal Deposit: D/2018/12603/564

Cover: © Primento

Digital conception by Primento, the digital partner of publishers.